ana & ANDREW

A Day at the Museum

by Christine Platt
illustrated by Sharon Sordo

Calico Kid
An Imprint of Magic Wagon
abdobooks.com

About the Author
Christine A. Platt is an author and scholar of African and African-American history. A beloved storyteller of the African diaspora, Christine enjoys writing historical fiction and non-fiction for people of all ages. You can learn more about her and her work at www.christineaplatt.com.

For the Ancestors. Thank you. —CP

For my parents, Thank you for your unyielding love and support. —SS

abdobooks.com

Published by Magic Wagon, a division of ABDO, PO Box 398166, Minneapolis, Minnesota 55439. Copyright © 2019 by Abdo Consulting Group, Inc. International copyrights reserved in all countries. No part of this book may be reproduced in any form without written permission from the publisher. Calico Kid™ is a trademark and logo of Magic Wagon.

Printed in the United States of America, North Mankato, Minnesota.
102018
012019

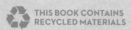
THIS BOOK CONTAINS RECYCLED MATERIALS

Written by Christine Platt
Illustrated by Sharon Sordo
Edited by Tamara L. Britton
Art Directed by Candice Keimig

Library of Congress Control Number: 2018947939

Publisher's Cataloging-in-Publication Data

Names: Platt, Christine, author. | Sordo, Sharon, illustrator.
Title: A day at the museum / by Christine Platt; illustrated by Sharon Sordo.
Description: Minneapolis, Minnesota : Magic Wagon, 2019. | Series: Ana & Andrew
Summary: It's a surprise visit! Ana & Andrew are excited when Grandma comes to stay. While she is there, the family tours the Smithsonian National Museum of African American History and Culture and learns about important African American achievements.
Identifiers: ISBN 9781532133527 (lib. bdg.) | ISBN 9781532134128 (ebook) | ISBN 9781532134425 (Read-to-me ebook)
Subjects: LCSH: Grandparents--Juvenile fiction. | Friendly visiting--Juvenile fiction. | National Museum of African American History and Culture (U.S.)--Juvenile fiction. | African American history--Juvenile fiction.
Classification: DDC [E]--dc23

Table of Contents

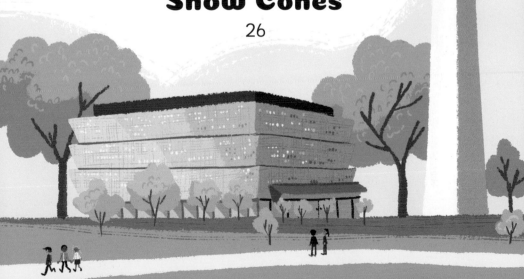

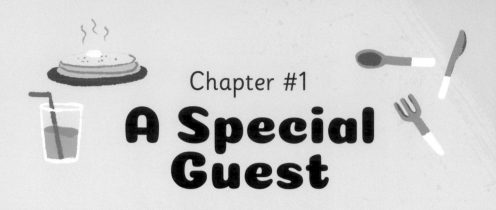

Chapter #1
A Special Guest

One rainy Saturday afternoon
Mama was in the kitchen making roti,
Andrew's favorite meal. As soon as
he smelled the curry, he did a wiggle-
dance and shouted, "Aye!"

5

"Today's lunch is special," Mama said. "We are having a guest."

"Who is it?" Ana asked.

There was a knock at the front door. Mama smiled. "Why don't you see for yourself?"

Ana and Andrew ran to the door and opened it. "Grandma!"

Grandma reached down to hug them both. Papa's mother was visiting from Georgia. Mama's mother, their Granny, lived in Trinidad.

"I'm so happy to see you," Ana said.

"Me too," said Andrew. "Can we bake cookies tonight?"

"Let Grandma inside first," Papa laughed.

"Of course, we can bake cookies." Grandma smiled. "But then we'll have to go straight to bed. We have a busy day tomorrow."

"We do?" Andrew asked. "What are we doing?"

"You haven't told them?" Grandma asked Mama and Papa.

"No," said Papa. "It's a surprise. Just like your visit."

"Tell us, Grandma," Ana demanded. "Or we are going to tickle you until you do."

Grandma was very ticklish. Andrew and Ana started tickling Grandma. Soon, everyone was laughing.

"I give up," Grandma laughed. "I'll tell you. We are going to a new museum. But that's all I'm going to say. You'll have to wait until tomorrow to find out more."

Museums have a lot of interesting things from the past, like dinosaur bones and old paintings. The new museum must be really special if Grandma came all the way from Georgia. Ana and Andrew couldn't wait to see what was inside.

Chapter #2
All
Aboard

Andrew and Ana finished tying their shoelaces.

"Is everyone ready?" Papa asked. "Make sure you're not forgetting anything."

"I'm ready." Andrew put on his favorite backpack.

"Me too." Ana held Sissy, her favorite dolly. They were dressed alike, as usual. Ana grabbed Grandma's hand so they could walk together.

"Alright," Papa said. "Let's go!"

They walked down the street to the Metro. Andrew and Ana loved to ride the train.

"Andrew, can you tell us how to get to the Smithsonian museums?" Mama asked.

Andrew looked closely at the Metro map. "We need to catch the train on the blue line. Then it's four stops from where we are now."

"Great job, Andrew," Papa said.

Andrew and Ana often visited museums in Washington, DC. The National Air and Space Museum was Andrew's favorite. He loved airplanes. Ana loved the National Museum of Natural History, especially the dinosaurs.

"Are you sure the museum we are going to is new?" Andrew asked.

"Yes," Grandma said. "We will be some of the first visitors."

"Yay!" Ana kissed Sissy. "Now that we're on our way, can you tell us what it's about?"

Grandma thought for a moment. "Well, it's about us."

"Us?" Andrew asked.

"Yes," Grandma said. "We are visiting the National Museum of African American History and Culture."

Chapter #3
Inside the Museum

The new museum was very tall and covered in gold. It sparkled in the sunshine. Andrew was very excited it was next to the Washington Monument. "Wow," Ana said. "It's so shiny and pretty."

"Welcome to the National Museum of African American History and Culture," a tour guide said.

"In all my years, I never imagined I'd see something so beautiful and important," Grandma whispered. She took a tissue from her purse and wiped her eyes.

"Are you okay?" Ana squeezed Grandma's hand tighter.

"Oh yes," Grandma said. "These are happy tears. Let's get started."

"Today you will learn how Africans were taken from their homeland and brought to America as slaves," a tour guide said.

"We learned about slavery in school," Andrew said. "That was a really sad time."

E PARADO
OF LIBERT

"Indeed it was," the tour guide agreed. "You will also learn about the great things African Americans have achieved since slavery. I hope you have a great time."

"Thank you," Grandma said.

Walking through the museum was like traveling through time. Andrew and Ana learned about civil rights leaders and the fight for equality. They also learned about the history of African Americans in the military and sports.

The art exhibit was beautiful, and Grandma even danced with them in the music exhibit. Andrew and Ana could not believe their ancestors had done so many amazing things.

"Wow," Andrew said. "Look!"

Everyone followed Andrew inside a room where a beautiful waterfall came from a bright circle in the ceiling.

"This room is where visitors reflect on African Americans' past and many achievements," a tour guide said.

"It's wonderful," Grandma whispered. Everyone stood quietly to honor African Americans. Andrew and Ana were very proud.

KENNEDY

Chapter #4
Snow Cones

People from all over the world loved to visit Washington, DC, and many were taking pictures. Papa took a picture of Andrew, Ana, and Grandma in front of the new museum. Then they went for a walk on the National Mall.

"Did everyone enjoy visiting the museum today?" Papa asked.

"Yes," Grandma, Mama, Andrew, and Ana said as they smiled.

"I am so proud of my ancestors," Ana said.

"Me too," Andrew agreed.

Andrew and Ana saw an ice cream truck. "Can we get snow cones?" Ana asked. "Please?"

"Yes," Mama said.

Andrew did a wiggle-dance and shouted, "Thank you!"

"Me and Sissy thank you, too!" Ana laughed.

Andrew and Ana went to the ice cream truck and ordered rainbow flavor. Papa, Mama, and Grandma ordered strawberry. They sat on the lawn at the National Mall, enjoying their snow cones in the sunshine.

"What are some of the exhibits you enjoyed?" Mama asked.

"I loved looking at the old dolls," Ana said. "Sissy did too."

"I liked the sports teams, especially baseball." Andrew smiled. "The old uniforms were kind of funny."

"Mama, what did you like the best?" Ana asked.

"I enjoyed seeing how people cooked years ago. It makes me love Granny's recipes even more."

"What did you like best, Papa?" Andrew asked.

"As a teacher, I enjoyed learning about African Americans' achievements. I cannot wait to tell my students."

"And what about you, Grandma?" Ana asked.

Grandma thought for a moment. "I loved everything. Especially enjoying a day at the museum with my family."

Andrew and Ana hugged Grandma. "Me too," they said. "Me too."